Always

Shine

Brightl

xoxo Krystian

SHINING SCARS

Krystian Leonard
illustrated by Lucas Kelly

Headline Kids
an imprint of Headline Books, Inc.
Terra Alta, WV

"For anyone who has come to see the
beauty in their scars and are as strong
as their stories behind them."

–Krystian

Shining Scars

by Krystian Leonard
illustrated by Lucas Kelly

copyright ©2013 Krystian Leonard

To order additional copies of this book,
for book publishing information,
or to contact the author:

Headline Books, Inc.
P.O. Box 52
Terra Alta, WV 26764
www.HeadlineKids.com

Tel: 800-570-5951
Email: mybook@headlinebooks.com

Headline Kids is an imprint of Headline Books

Illustrations by Lucas Kelly
www.designmarie.com

ISBN-13: 978-0-937467-72-4

Library of Congress Control Number: 2013938674

PRINTED IN THE UNITED STATES OF AMERICA

Once upon a time there was
a little star named Eugene.

Little Eugene loved to see how fast
he could fly in the night time sky.

The little star's mom warned
him not to go too fast!

She didn't want
him to get hurt...

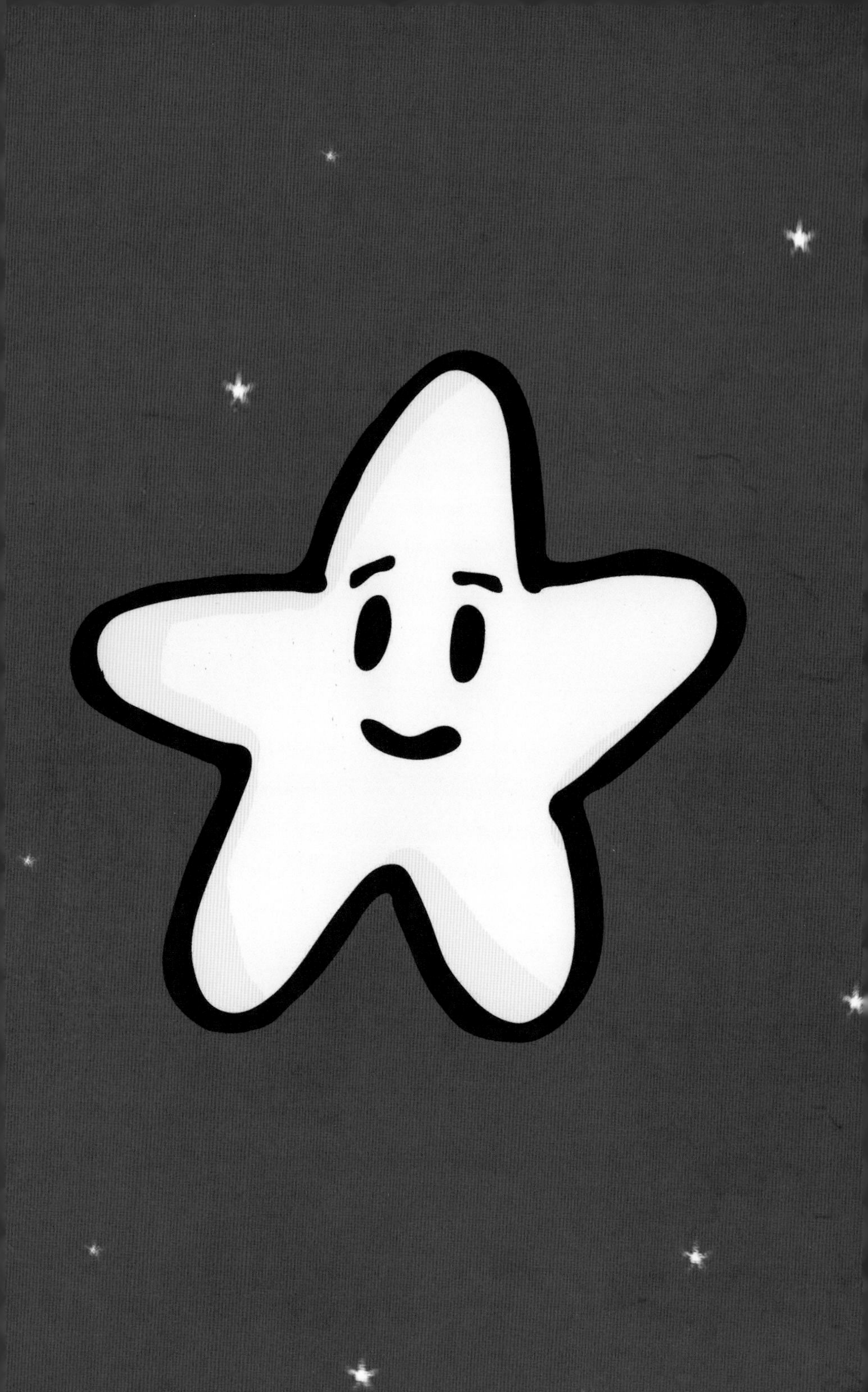

But the little star didn't
listen to his mom.

And one day he flew across
the sky too fast and fell!

The little star fell on
his head and got a boo-boo!

He cried to his mom
while she held him tight.

She looked into his eyes
and told him everything
will be all right.

She took little Eugene to the Galaxy Hospital...
where they took special care.

When they were done
Eugene felt better and was happy
to go home.

But Eugene was scared
about his new scar and didn't
want his friends to know.
His mom told him not to worry,
his scar would shine bright!

After their talk,
he wasn't scared anymore.
So the little star fell
sound asleep that night.

When Eugene woke up
the next morning he was so surprised!
His little scar shined extra bright!

Little Eugene suddenly
wasn't afraid of his scar and
couldn't wait to show his friends
his shining new spot!

Eugene's friend's asked
him lots of questions that day.
And he never gave it a thought.

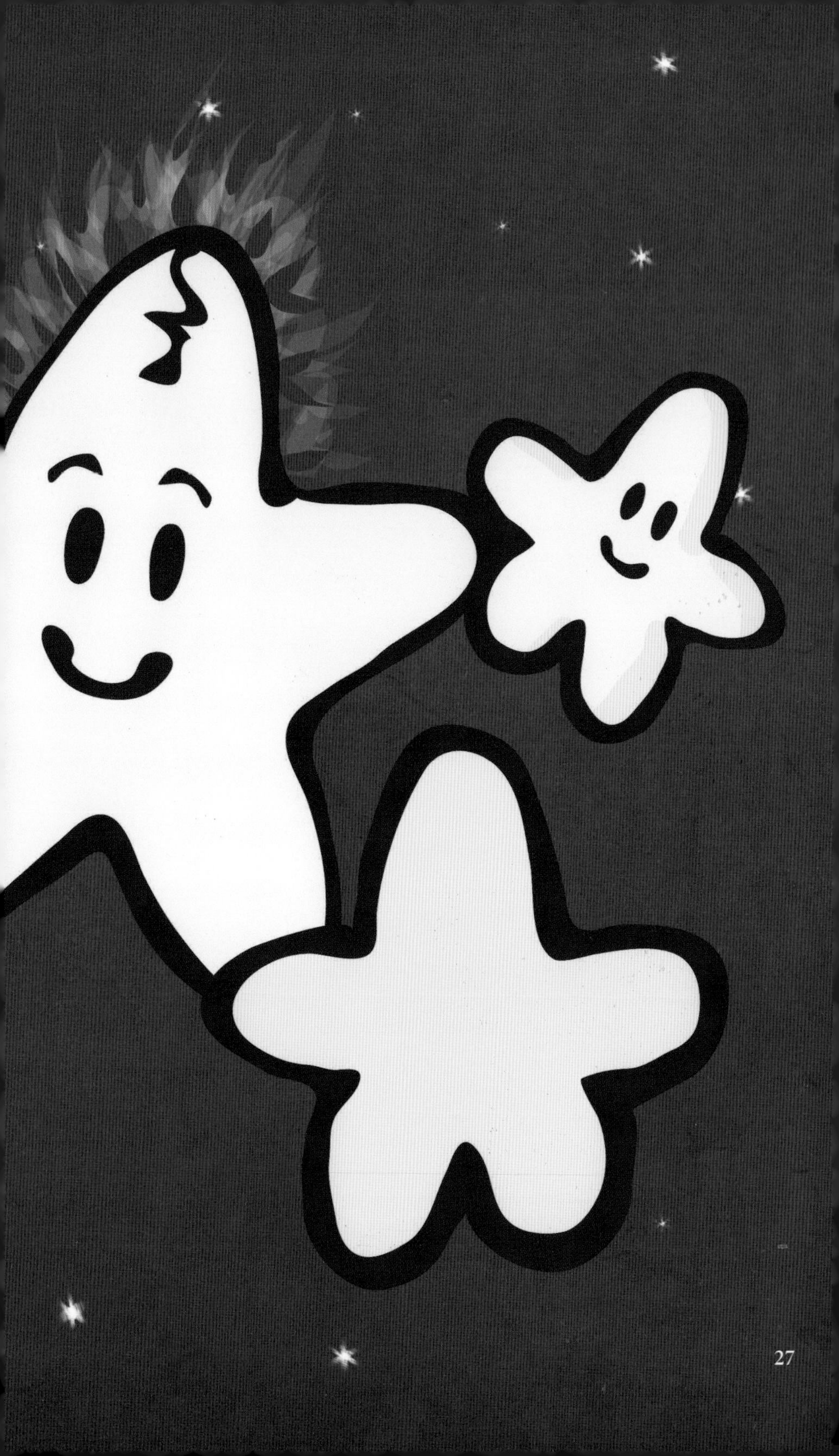

He wanted his friends to
know everything about his scar and
to them he taught—kindness and caring—
and to see scars in a different light.

He taught about how it glows!
He taught about how it shines!
And all his little friends said...
Look at mine!

Krystian Leonard is a sophomore in high school and entered her first pageant at age 14. She wrote Shining Scars as a way to reach out to children healing with visible scars. Krystian developed and created her own nonprofit organization Shining S.C.A.R.S. at age 15 as a result of the scars she endured. She spends countless hours volunteering and promoting her organization as well as competing in pageantry.

Growing up she experienced firsthand the trials and self-esteem issues associated with visible scars. She had her first stitches, resulting in a scar, at age 4. It was above her lip and she wouldn't smile for pictures and was embarrassed going to preschool. When she was 7, she had her first surgical procedure to remove a lipoma growth in her thigh, leaving a 9" scar. At the age of 12, she had surgery to remove a large birth mark on her lower back as a preventative measure, leaving behind a 5" scar. Enduring another surgery and yet another large scar was one of the worst experiences for her budding self-esteem. Going to the pool or wearing shorts was always a guarantee she would be asked 'what's that?' or 'what happened to you?' This was hard for her at first— however she learned to accept and overcome her fear and to share her story. The more she talked about her scars, the better she felt about them. This was her inspiration behind her organization Shining S.C.A.R.S.

You can find out more about Krystian and Shining S.C.A.R.S. by visiting her website at www.ShiningScars.org or by email at ShiningScars@gmail. com. This website has been designed to assist both children and teens with the healing process. By creating a positive and character-building organization, Krystian's goal is to build a community to inform and to assist people with the healing process associated with disfiguring scars.

Krystian has continually proven that beauty is more than skin deep and hopes to help others heal so they, too, can say "no matter what my scars say to you, they hold a meaning of trength and haracter, showing I have ccepted who I am and prove I can ise above the tigma."